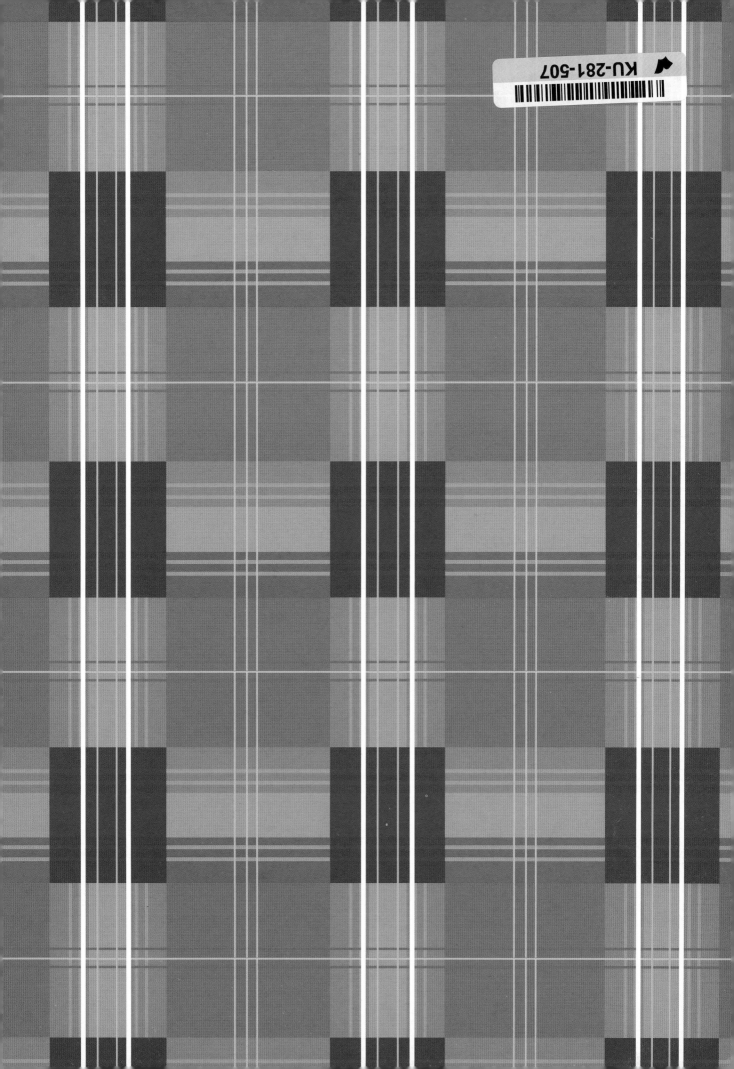
KU-281-507

PUFFIN BOOKS

Published by the Penguin Group
Penguin Books Ltd, 80 Strand, London WC2R 0RL, England
Penguin Putnam Inc., 375 Hudson Street, New York, New York 10014, USA
Penguin Books Australia Ltd, 250 Camberwell Road, Camberwell, Victoria 3124, Australia
Penguin Books Canada Ltd, 10 Alcorn Avenue, Toronto, Ontario, Canada M4V 3B2
Penguin Books India (P) Ltd, 11 Community Centre, Panchsheel Park, New Delhi – 110 017, India
Penguin Books (NZ) Ltd, Cnr Rosedale and Airborne Roads, Albany, Auckland, New Zealand
Penguin Books (South Africa) (Pty) Ltd, 24 Sturdee Avenue, Rosebank 2196, South Africa

Penguin Books Ltd, Registered Offices: 80 Strand, London WC2R 0RL, England

www.penguin.com

First published 2002
1

Stuart Little 2 TM & © Columbia Pictures Industries, Inc.
Interior design by Gavin Morris
Unit photography by Peter Iovino
CG imagery by Sony Pictures Imageworks
Published by arrangement with HarperCollins Publishers, Inc., New York, N.Y., U.S.A
All rights reserved

Made and printed in Italy by Printer Trento Srl

Except in the United States of America, this book is sold subject to the condition that it shall not, by way of trade or otherwise,
be lent, re-sold, hired out, or otherwise circulated without the publisher's prior consent in any form of binding or cover other than
that in which it is published and without a similar condition including
this condition being imposed on the subsequent purchaser

British Library Cataloguing in Publication Data
A CIP catalogue record for this book is available from the British Library

ISBN 0–141–31479–6

STUART LITTLE 2™

The Storybook

Adapted by Julie Michaels
Based on the screenplay by Bruce Joel Rubin
Based on the story by Douglas Wick and Bruce Joel Rubin

COLUMBIA PICTURES PRESENTS A RED WAGON AND FRANKLIN/WATERMAN PRODUCTION A FILM BY ROB MINKOFF STARRING: GEENA DAVIS "STUART LITTLE 2" HUGH LAURIE AND JONATHAN LIPNICKI MUSIC BY ALAN SILVESTRI EXECUTIVE PRODUCERS JEFF FRANKLIN AND STEVE WATERMAN ROB MINKOFF GAIL LYON JASON CLARK BASED UPON CHARACTERS FROM THE BOOK "STUART LITTLE" BY E.B. WHITE STORY BY DOUGLAS WICK AND BRUCE JOEL RUBIN SCREENPLAY BY BRUCE JOEL RUBIN PRODUCED BY LUCY FISHER AND DOUGLAS WICK DIRECTED BY ROB MINKOFF COLUMBIA PICTURES

StuartLittle.com

PUFFIN BOOKS

Chapter 1

Stuart's New Friend

Stuart Little was part of a loving family.
The Littles lived all together in the big city.

Stuart lived with his mother; father; brother, George; and baby sister, Martha. Stuart was the littlest Little.

Even though Stuart was little, he liked to play the games that other boys his age played, including football.

"It's going to be great!" cheered Stuart before his first game.

A big breakfast would help Stuart be ready to play. Of course, most breakfasts were big to Stuart!

At the football game, Stuart was happy when his coach finally put him on the field to play. Stuart was ready to help his team.

But when Stuart ran on to the field, the ball hit him so hard that he stuck to it and went flying into the goal.

"Do I get an assist?" groaned Stuart.

Mrs Little worried that Stuart would get hurt. "He looks so small out there – so lacking in 'bigness'. Does he really have to play football?" she asked.

"We have to give him room to grow," said Mr Little.

Mrs Little thought Stuart had found a nice, safe hobby in building toy models. Stuart and his brother had already built a boat and a car. Now they were building a plane.

But something went wrong . . .

"I'm in the air!" cried Stuart, as the plane

suddenly took off.

Stuart flew through his house and straight out the door. His worried family hurried after him.

The plane took Stuart into a nearby park.
"Mayday! Mayday!" cried Stuart. "Nuns
at twelve o'clock."

Stuart tried to keep calm. *There must be some way to land*, he thought to himself.

Stuart found a way – he flew straight into a thick bush. *Swoosh-smash-crash!* Luckily, Stuart was not hurt.

Mr Little tried to make Stuart feel better. "The thing about being a Little is you can always see the bright side," he said. "Every cloud has a silver lining."

Every cloud? wondered Stuart.

Happily, Stuart's car was still working. *Beep-beep!*

While he was driving home from school one day . . . *Crash!* A little bird fell from the sky into his car.

She was being chased by an angry falcon.
Stuart and his speedy red roadster rescued the
unexpected passenger.

The bird yelled at the falcon as they drove off, "Eat my feathers, you vile buzzard!"

Zoom-zoom!

Stuart's expert driving helped them escape the falcon.

"We did it!" cried the grateful bird. "Or should I say, *you* did it?"

"Yeah!" said Stuart proudly. "I did."

Stuart introduced himself and brought the bird home. Her name was Margalo. Stuart tended her hurt wing. He had made a new friend.

At the Little house, Margalo settled into
a comfy jewellery box.

"I'll just stay till my wing heals," said
Margalo.

"Stay as long as you like," offered Mrs
Little.

All the Littles were very welcoming, except for Snowbell.

Guests are like fish, he thought. *After two days, they start to stink!*

Chapter 2

Missing Margalo

Margalo fitted in well with the Little family. She liked to play games and sing songs as much as they did.

Stuart was happy to have a friend of his own – especially one who was his own size.

"You're as big as you feel," Margalo told him.

Stuart began to believe her.

One day, Mrs Little was washing the dishes when she noticed she was missing her diamond ring.

"It could have gone down the drain!" she cried.

Stuart wanted to go and look for the ring, but Mr Little was worried.

"I don't know, Stuart. It's awfully dark down there," he said.

"Come on, Dad, let me try," said Stuart.

Mr Little fashioned a hook and string to lower brave Stuart into the drain.

"How is it down there so far?" asked George.

"Wet," replied Stuart.

Suddenly, the string holding the hook broke. *Ker-plunk!* Stuart was trapped at the bottom of the drain.

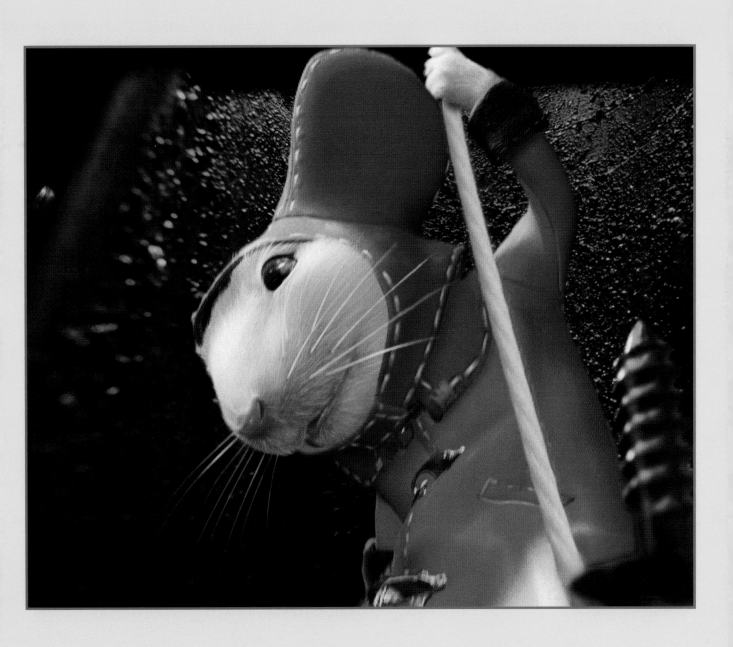

The Little family searched the kitchen but could not find any more string to rescue Stuart. Then Margalo opened the clasp on Mrs Little's necklace and lowered it down the drain. Stuart grabbed the necklace, and Margalo lifted him to safety.

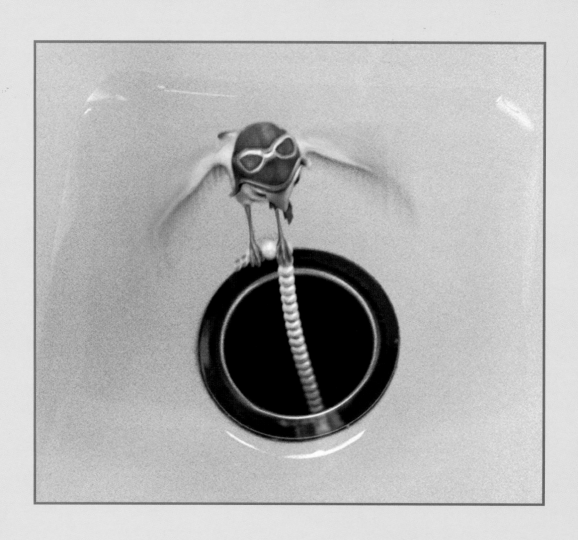

Hooray! All the Littles were happy to have Stuart back.

"Margalo, you're the best friend I ever had," said Stuart.

Margalo felt bad. She knew where the ring really was, but she couldn't tell Stuart.

The next day, the Littles called a plumber
to check the drain, but the ring was not there.

Then Margalo went missing too!

"I can't find her anywhere," said Stuart.

"Maybe she just felt it was time to go,"
Mr Little said gently.

Stuart did not believe that could be true.

That night, Stuart could not sleep.

"I think I know what happened to Margalo," Stuart told George. "The falcon got her!"

Stuart knew he had to save Margalo.

"Stuart . . ." George said awkwardly. "She's just a bird."

"No, George," said Stuart. "She's my friend. And when you're friends with Stuart Little, you're friends for life."

Stuart convinced Snowbell to join his adventure in the big city.

Down a dirty, dark alley, Stuart and Snowbell found Monty.

Monty was just the type of rough-and-tumble streetcat who would know where the falcon lived.

"Falcon? The jewel thief?" cried Monty.
"You don't want to find him!"

Stuart persisted and, finally, Monty told
them that Falcon lived across the park at the top
of the Pishkin Building.

Stuart quickly phoned George to let his brother know where he was going. Then Stuart and Snowbell made their way to the Pishkin Building. But how could they get up to the top?

"I'll think of something," Stuart told Snowbell. And that's just what he did.

Stuart attached a small paper cup to a balloon. Then he boarded the cup. Up, up, up he floated.

"You can do it!" called Snowbell. To himself, he added, "This has 'fiasco' written all over it."

Stuart carefully stepped out of the paper cup and on to the roof.

"Margalo, are you up here?" he called.

Suddenly, Falcon appeared. Margalo was with him.

"She does what I tell her," Falcon growled. Stuart could not believe that Margalo worked for Falcon!

Falcon did not give Margalo time to explain. He grabbed Stuart in his talons.

"Don't hurt him, Falcon!" pleaded Margalo.

Falcon ignored her. He carried Stuart to the edge of the building . . . and let go.

"No!" cried Margalo.

Far below, Stuart landed in the back of a rubbish truck.

Chapter 3

Stuart to the Rescue

Stuart wound up on a stinky, slimy rubbish barge.

"I know a Little is always supposed to see a silver lining," Stuart told himself, but this time it was hard for him to believe. "Maybe this means I'm not really a Little. Maybe I'm Stuart . . . Nobody."

Stuart felt about as low and little as he ever had before.

Then suddenly . . . the silver lining! Buried in the rubbish was Stuart's aeroplane – the one George had thrown away!

Could Stuart make it fly again?

While Stuart was stuck on the rubbish
barge, George finally told his parents that
Stuart had gone to the Pishkin Building
to save Margalo.

The Littles jumped into a taxi to
search for Stuart.

Everyone was worried about the middle
Little. Mr Little tried to stay hopeful.

"We don't have to assume the worst," he
said. "After all, it's not the Little way."

Far above the worried family, Margalo told Falcon, "I'm through doing what you tell me to do. I'm leaving you, Falcon. Forever!"

Margalo grabbed Mrs Little's ring – she had stolen it for Falcon. Now she was going to take it back where it belonged.

Angrily, Falcon flew after Margalo. He was about to grab her when he heard . . . *Putt-putt-putt!* Stuart scooped Margalo into his plane!

"Stuart, you're alive!" Margalo cried happily.

"So far," said Stuart.

Falcon screeched after them at top speed.
Stuart flew wildly, diving and weaving. It was
no use. Falcon was gaining on them.

Then Stuart had an idea. First he got
Margalo safely out of the plane. Next Stuart
headed his plane straight towards Falcon!
Bird and plane flew faster and faster towards
a collision.

Just before impact, Stuart used the diamond in his mother's ring to reflect sunlight into Falcon's eyes. A dazed Falcon crashed into the plane, just after Stuart had leaped out.

"Bye-bye, birdbrain!" called Stuart, using a tablecloth he had in his rucksack as a parachute. Falcon fell to the ground. He never bothered anyone again.

"Stuart!" cheered the happy Little family, who had arrived at the park just in time to witness his heroics.

Margalo returned Mrs Little's ring.

"I took it," she confessed.

"And now she's giving it back," Stuart said kindly.

"I'm just glad to have all of you back," added Mrs Little. When Snowbell found the happy group, the family was complete.

Stuart and Margalo were good friends. They knew each other well. When the summer ended, Stuart noticed how much Margalo wanted to head south with the other birds. He urged her to follow her dream.

"I'll miss you, Stuart," she said before flying off.

Watching her go, Mr Little wondered out loud, "What's the silver lining this time?"

"She'll be back in the spring," Stuart answered.

Stuart smiled. However far Margalo flew, Stuart would always carry her friendship in his great big Little heart.

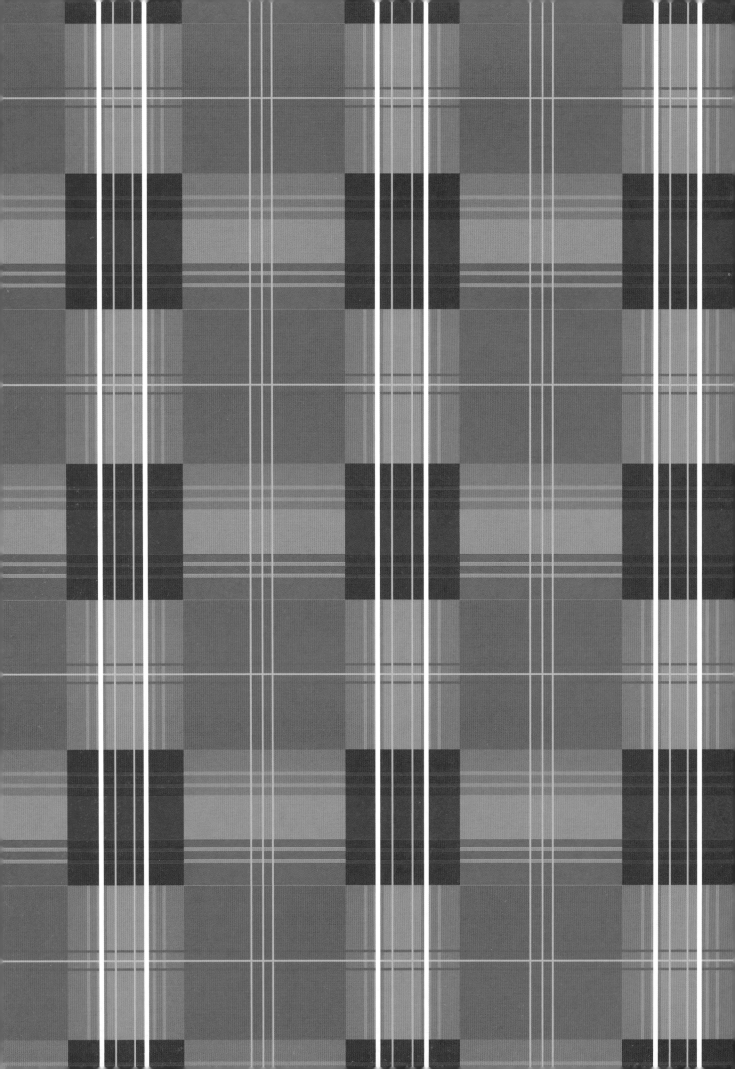